This book belongs to

_____

First published in Great Britain by HarperCollins Publishers Ltd in 1995.
ISBN 0 00 761369 5 Text and illustrations copyright © Mark Burgess 1995
The author asserts the moral right to be identified as the author of this work. A CIP catalogue record for this title is available
from the British Library. All rights reserved. No part of the publication may be reproduced, stored in a retrieval system, or
transmitted in any form or by any means, electronic, mechanical, photocopying, recording or otherwise, without the prior permission
of HarperCollins Publishers Ltd, 77-85 Fulham Palace Road, Hammersmith, London W6 8JB Printed and bound in Singapore

Teddy and Rabbit's
Birthday Surprise

Mark Burgess

Collins

An Imprint of HarperCollinsPublishers

One morning Teddy and Rabbit
were woken up by someone
knocking on the shop door.
"Who's that?" said Teddy, sleepily.
"It's Elephant," said Rabbit.

Teddy and Rabbit's Shop

"Isn't the shop open?" said Elephant.
"It's not time yet," said Teddy.
"Don't worry," said Rabbit.
"We can open it specially for you."

"Now then, what do you want?"
asked Teddy.

"Oh dear..." said Elephant.
"I can't remember."

"Well, what did
you want the
things for?"
asked Rabbit.

"A surprise,"
whispered
Elephant.
"I'm going to...

...A...

...A...

...ACHOOO!" sneezed Elephant.

Elephant took out his hanky.

"Of course!" he said.

"I wanted some cherries and... err..."
"Some sugar?" suggested Teddy.

"Yes!" said Elephant. "And some
flour, some butter and..."

"Some eggs?" suggested Rabbit.
"That's right!" said Elephant.

"Is that everything?" asked Teddy.
"Yes, I think so," said Elephant.
"Thank you. Bye-bye."

Teddy and Rabbit's Shop

Later that day Elephant came back.
"Hello," said Teddy. "Did you
forget something?"
"Not this time," said Elephant.
"I remembered it's your birthday."

"Oh, thank you," said Teddy.
"Cherry cake! My favourite.
And just in time for tea."